Walk With Me

Walk With Me

by Naomi Danis
Illustrated by Jacqueline Rogers

SCHOLASTIC INC.

Cartwheel B·O·O·K·S ®

New York Toronto London Auckland Sydney
Mexico City New Delhi Hong Kong

For Gil, Sophie, Ezra, and Talya
—N.D.

Dedicated with love to Emma
—J.R.

ISBN 0-439-29693-5

Text copyright © 1995 by Naomi Davis.
Illustrations copyright © 1995 by Jacqueline Rogers.
All rights reserved.
Published by Scholastic Inc.
by arrangement with CARTWHEEL BOOKS,
a registered trademark of Scholastic Inc.
SCHOLASTIC and associated logos are trademarks and/or
registered trademarks of Scholastic Inc.

12 11 10 9 8 7 6 5   4 5 6/0

Printed in the U.S.A.   08

First Scholastic printing, May 2001

feel
the warming
morning
mellow
yellow
sun

feel
the cool
of the blue sky
breeze

hear
the leaves
rustle
restless
in the trees

hold my hand
walk with me

wait
stop
for red
steady

dog barks
tail wagging
happy
cat quietly
tiptoes
by

wait till
green
tells us go

at last
the park
grassy
green

with
swings
slides
seesaws
climbing things
benches

wide-open space
let go now
run around
in circles
arms out
lift off

twittering birds
soar away
afraid
of your stamping feet

bend down
look closely
see ants
hauling crumbs
crawling quickly
somewhere away

be kind
let them go

boo!
guess who

suddenly
I catch you
before
you can splash
into a muddy
puddle

I lift you up
we stare
into the dark water
who's there?
you are
I am
see you
see me
say hello
to our
reflections

come along
meander wander
dawdle dillydally
see
something beautiful
a butterfly
reach for it
chase it
fly along
leap jump bump
down up again
off again

then tired
slowed down
heavy now
legs won't go now
carry me please
carry me
tired now

oh no
walk with me
keep going
you can do it
yes you can
hold my hand

what have you got?
open tight fists
full of treasures
a feather
a pebble
a twig
a petal

walk with me
let's count
one house
two houses
three houses
behind every door
someone to smile at
say hello
wave good-bye

finally
our house
open the door
go inside
climb into my lap
ready for a nap
rock together
rest together
happy
that we walked
together